First American Trade Edition 1994 by Kane/Miller
Book Publishers, Brooklyn, New York & La Jolla, California

Originally published in Spanish under the title *El Sapo
Distraído* by Ediciones Ekaré–Banco del Libro, Caracas Venezuela.
Copyright © 1988 Ediciones Ekaré–Banco del Libro.
English translation copyright © 1994 by Harcourt Brace & Company

All rights reserved. For information contact:
Kane/Miller Book Publishers
P.O. Box 310529, Brooklyn, NY 11231-0529

Library of Congress Cataloging-in-Publication Data

Rondón, Javier
  [Sapo distraído. English]
  The absent-minded toad / by Javier Rondón; translated by Kathryn
Corbett; illustrated by Marcela Cabrera.—1st American trade ed.

  Summary: A toad becomes so absorbed in the act of going to the
  market that he forgets to buy anything.
  [1. Toads—Fiction. 2. Markets—Fiction. 3. Stories in rhyme.]
  I. Corbett, Kathryn. II. Cabrera, Marcela, ill. III. Title.
  PZ8.3.R665Ab 1994   94-14407
  ISBN 0-916291-53-7

Printed and bound in Singapore by Tien Wah Press Pte. Ltd.
1 2 3 4 5 6 7 8 9 10

The Absent-Minded Toad

Javier Rondón

Illustrated by Marcela Cabrera

Translated by Kathryn Corbett

A CRANKY NELL BOOK

Kane/Miller Book Publishers

Brooklyn, New York & La Jolla, California

A toad

of rainbow colors—

Orange, green,

and brown—

Made out a list

one morning

To take with him

to town.

Butter for tortillas,

Jam to put on toast.

He looked around his kitchen

For what he needed most.

A flower in his blue cap,

Around his leg a bell.

He smiled into his mirror.

He did look very well!

Then off he went to market

Hop, hop, hop!

Looking in the windows

Of every kind of shop.

He stopped on the corner

Where the fruit seller sells

Fruits of many colors—

Oh, what lovely smells!

What a crowd of people
Dressed in their best!
Choosing cheese and eggs
Fresh from the nest.

"Tomatoes from my garden!"
The tomato seller said.
"Here, lady, try one—
Fresh and ripe and red!

He hopped round the market

Almost all the day.

In all that crowd of people

Toad nearly lost his way.

At last he got home safely

And put his feet up.

He drank some warm milk

From his old blue cup.

He went for bread and butter

And then he said, "Oh, my!"

I hopped around the market,

But nothing did I buy!"